Voices
in St. Augustine

Also by Jane R. Wood

Adventures on Amelia Island:
A Pirate, A Princess, and Buried Treasure

Trouble on the St. Johns River

Ghosts on the Coast:
A Visit to Savannah and the Low Country

To Ava + Elena,
Keep Reading!

Voices
in St. Augustine

Jane R. Wood

Jane R Wood

Florida Kids Press, Inc.   ◆   Jacksonville, FL

Publisher's Cataloging-In-Publication Data
(Prepared by The Donohue Group, Inc.)

Wood, Jane R.
Voices in St. Augustine / Jane R. Wood
– 4th ed. – p. : ill. ; cm.
Includes bibliographical references

ISBN: 978-0-9792304-5-5

1. Teenage boys-Fiction. 2. Saint Augustine (Fla.)–History–Fiction.
3. Adventure fiction.

I. Title
PS3573.059 V65 2004
813.6

Illustrations, cover design and graphic design by Elizabeth A. Blacker.

Published through:
Florida Kids Press, Inc., 11802 Magnolia Falls Drive
Jacksonville, FL 32258
904-268-9572

www.janewoodbooks.com

Printed and bound in the USA.

To Jonathan and Brian

Acknowledgements

Voices in St. Augustine is my first book. As with many things, the first one is usually the hardest. I was fortunate to have many people who helped me bring it to publication.

My family and friends were the first to see the manuscript. My husband, Terry, read it first. His support has been unwavering from the beginning and has made all the difference for me.

Then it went to my sons, Jonathan and Brian, who were the models for my characters of Joey and Bobby. My sister Priscilla, my daughter-in-law Jennifer, and my nieces Emily and Lindsey, who became the character Katy, were next. Linda Smigaj, a very talented 4th grade teacher, gave valuable feedback. All of their comments were very helpful and their enthusiasm was especially encouraging.

Then I turned to the professionals. Dan and Mary Hubley steered me down the path of publishing a first book. Edits were done by Mary Hubley and communications consultant Gena Jerozal. My graphic designer, Elizabeth A. Blacker, worked her magic on the cover, the illustrations, and the layout. I relied on her talent, insights and advice heavily, and she never let me down.

I share any compliments this book receives with all of these people. I couldn't do it without them!

Chapter 1
The History Project

"Mom! He got into my stuff again," Joey yelled. "Make him stay out of my room!"

"I didn't touch his stuff," Bobby argued. "I was only looking for MY batting glove. He's always using MINE, just because he can't find HIS. He doesn't even have a game today!"

"So what do you care? Neither do you!"

"That doesn't matter. It's MINE!"

Life in the Johnson household was never dull with two energetic boys, a sassy little sister, and a hyperactive dog. The television was always on. There were several pairs of shoes scattered on the floor in the family room, and there was usually something sticky on the refrigerator door.

Joey Johnson was thirteen and in the eighth grade. He felt much more mature than his nine-year-old brother.

Bobby, who was still in elementary school, was envious of his older brother and could hardly wait to get to middle school to try out for the school baseball team.

"I'm sure I'll make it. I'm already better than some of those guys who are older than me," he said.

And he was right. Bobby made the All-Star team every year in Little League. He usually led his team in homeruns and was a ruthless shortstop. The other players on his team knew to pay attention when a ball was hit to Bobby, because there was a good chance he would relay it to one of them. He loved to go for a double play.

"When I get to middle school, I'm going to set some new school records," he said to his little sister.

"I know you will, Bobby," five-year-old Katy said. "You're always the best player on your team."

Katy was his biggest fan. In fact, she adored both of her brothers. They teased her sometimes, like brothers do, but they were her heroes.

Joey was glad when he started middle school because he no longer had to attend the same school as his younger brother and sister. It made him feel more independent.

It also meant riding the school bus, which he hated, especially on hot Florida days when it smelled of sweaty bodies. But sometimes it had its advantages. Once on a Monday morning one of the kids on the bus mentioned a current events assignment he had forgotten.

"Hey, Joey. What kind of news story are you going to talk about today in Mr. Davis's class?" a boy asked.

"I'm trying to decide which article to use," he lied. "There were lots of good stories in Sunday's paper."

Fortunately, he had the copy of Sunday's sports page with him. He always had a sports page with him in case there was a substitute teacher in one of his classes. Subs meant free time and a chance to talk to some of the other boys in his class who shared his love of baseball.

They would discuss their favorite teams and players, although none of the other kids studied the box scores as closely as Joey did. He played *Fantasy Baseball*, so he liked to keep track of the statistics of his favorite players. Plus, math was his favorite subject. He enjoyed playing with the numbers almost as much as he enjoyed fielding grounders.

He also liked to wave the sports page at Jeremiah, the school custodian who was a big New York Yankees fan.

"The Red Sox are going to take 'em this year, Jeremiah."

"We'll see," Jeremiah would say.

They had been having these exchanges ever since Joey started attending the school. Joey first met Jeremiah when he tried to open his assigned locker during school orientation two years earlier and found it would not budge. Jeremiah was sent to investigate the problem and determined it was indeed stuck. While he tried numerous maneuvers to pry it open, Joey noticed a Yankees baseball cap stuck in Jeremiah's back pocket.

"Don't tell me you're a fan of those rotten Yankees. They're bums!" Joey said.

"I've been a Yankees fan for longer than you've been on this earth," Jeremiah said.

After that day, a friendly rivalry had developed. Jeremiah would tip his cap when he passed Joey in the hallway, and Joey would say some smart-aleck comment about the Yankees.

But Jeremiah's friendship couldn't help him now with this social studies assignment. Joey's group had been assigned local news, so he had to find an article on the sports page that had something to do with his city. Lucky for him, there was a story about a professional baseball player from their hometown whose baseball days were over because of an eye injury.

"Because he went to college and got a business degree, he'll be able to get a job after his baseball career has ended," Joey reported to the class when it was his turn.

Mr. Davis was so impressed with Joey's observation that he spent another ten minutes lecturing the class on the importance of getting a good education. Joey felt like he'd hit a homerun with that assignment.

After that, things went downhill. Mr. Davis announced they had a history project due in six weeks. The whole class groaned. Joey's stomach started to churn. He hated history. Well, he didn't actually hate it, but he didn't see any use for it. *Spending any amount of time working on a project about things from the past is a big waste of time,* he thought.

He considered recycling the report he had done on Thomas Jefferson in the fifth grade when they had studied the American presidents, but Mr. Davis wanted their projects to have some local historic connection. Why hadn't he done his report on Andrew Jackson? After all, he lived in Jacksonville, which had been named after Old Hickory himself. That would have worked out nicely. But he hadn't done that!

This assignment only increased his dislike for social studies. *History stinks,* he thought.

Chapter 2
Family Values

When Joey got home from school that afternoon, his grandparents' car was in the driveway. If Grandma was there after school, it usually meant she was baking something. His favorite was chocolate chip cookies. Grandma had learned from experience to get the cookies into the oven before the kids got home or else more cookie dough got eaten than got baked.

Katy was in the kitchen with Grandma, standing on a chair to reach the counter. She had cookie dough everywhere. She had butter on her fingers, flour in her hair, and a huge grin on her face.

"Look what I made," she said while pointing to a cookie sheet on the kitchen counter.

"It's a super-duper tasty chocolate concession."

"You mean confection," Joey replied.

7

"Yes, dear," Grandma said to Katy. "Confection is what you meant. That means something sweet."

"Whatever," Katy said with a wave of her hand. "It's what's inside that is important."

Grandma smiled.

"Looks delicious, Katy," Joey said as he grabbed a warm cookie. "Where's Grandpa?"

"He's outside with Bobby. They're repairing a hole in the fence so Max won't get out again," Grandma said.

"Oh, that ought to be good. Bobby doesn't know how to fix anything!"

"Well, that's how you learn. Your grandfather is an expert at repairing things. Why don't you go see if you can help? We'll be done here in a minute. I've got some bread in the oven, and I'm going to start dinner shortly. Your mom had a late interview, so I'm the chief cook today."

Jennifer Johnson wrote stories for local magazines and newspapers. On the afternoons when she couldn't be there when the kids got home from school, their grandparents would "hold down the fort" for her, as their grandfather liked to say.

Joey gingerly lifted another hot cookie from the cooling rack and headed outside.

"Hey, Joe-Joe. How was school?" his grandfather asked, as he was getting ready to nail a new board to the old fence.

Joey hated being called Joe-Joe, but he didn't have the heart to tell his grandfather that. He tolerated it and hoped that he would never say it in front of his friends.

"It was OK, except for social studies. I've got to do a history project, and I hate history."

"Don't say that. History was one of my favorite subjects. In fact, it still is."

"Yeah, you're always watching *The History Channel*, Grandpa," Bobby said.

"You bet. So what are you going to do your project on?"

"I don't have a clue. It has to be something with a local connection. Where am I going to find something interesting that happened here?"

"There's a pretty good exhibit downtown at the Museum of Science and History. I'd be glad to take you there on Saturday and maybe you'll see something that interests you."

"I can tell you right now — NOTHING interests me."

"Don't make up your mind so fast. You'd be surprised how fascinating history can be. If you just give it a chance, you might stumble onto something exciting."

"I'd rather stumble over Mr. Davis in a coma," Joey said sarcastically. "It's not due for six weeks yet, so I've got some time to dig up something."

"Well, while you're thinking about that, come over here and I'll show you how to take care of this fence."

Joey held a board in place while his grandfather nailed it. Then Grandpa gave Bobby instructions on how to measure the next one for cutting. While the three of them were focused on the finer points of home repair, Max slipped through the fence opening that was not covered and headed for parts unknown. Bobby caught a glimpse of his reddish tail as the dog bolted through the hole.

"He's out again!"

Both boys ran into the house. Bobby hollered, "Battle stations. Max is on the loose!"

Joey went to the pantry for a handful of dog treats. Katy looked for the leash, while Bobby raced through the front door heading in the direction Max had gone. Grandma went to the laundry room to find the old beach towel they used for Max's bath. He would probably come back dirty, smelly and wet. Dinner would have to wait.

Bobby saw the dachshund heading straight for the busy road that led into their neighborhood. He started chasing the dog just as his mother turned the corner in her minivan and spotted the runaway pooch. She stopped the van, scooped up the dog, and signaled a thumbs-up to Bobby.

Joey caught up with his brother and said, "It's a good thing he has short legs."

"And he's lucky we got to him before he got into some real trouble. It looks like he's escaped getting a bath, too. We ought to give him one just to teach him a lesson," Bobby said.

They returned to the house where they were greeted

11

with a mouth-watering aroma coming from the kitchen. Grandma had just taken the bread out of the oven.

"As soon as it cools, you can have a piece. It's still too hot to cut. In the meantime, go wash up. Dinner will be ready in a shake."

Their grandparents liked to use words like that: "chief cook," "in a shake," and "hold down the fort." They were from a different era. Even though those phrases weren't used anymore, they sounded familiar to Joey and his brother and sister, because they had been hearing them all of their lives.

Maybe that's what history was all about — that connection from one era to the next. Joey would have to think about that later. Right now, all he could think about was warm bread oozing with melted butter. As he picked up a slice and buttered it, he wondered if bread tasted this good to the early pioneers.

Why were these strange thoughts about the early settlers suddenly popping into his head? Things from the past had nothing to do with him.

Chapter 3
A Visit to St. Augustine

After a hectic week, Saturday finally arrived. Katy was up early watching cartoons in a zombie-like state. Bobby was still asleep when Joey stumbled out of his room. He went straight to the newspaper to find the sports page. His mother was reading the food section and making a grocery list.

"What have you got planned for today?" she asked.

He hesitated. Should he make up something quickly or should he tell the truth? The truth was he planned to spend most of the morning on his computer, and then he wanted to watch the Red Sox game on TV that afternoon. It was the end of the summer and every game counted now in the race to get to the World Series. He knew the Red Sox didn't stand a chance this year, but they were HIS team.

"I've got things to do," he finally replied.

"I've got to go to St. Augustine to do some research for a story on southern architecture. I was hoping you'd come with me. I hate to drive down there alone."

"What about Bobby or Katy?"

"Katy's been invited to a birthday party for one of the girls in her dance class and Bobby's going fishing with the Lees. Besides, it's Saturday and you need to get out. You shouldn't stay in the house all day."

Ugh, thought Joey. *I'm not going to get out of this one.*

"How long will it take? I'd like to see the Red Sox game at 3:00."

Jennifer knew better than to compete with the Red Sox. In fact, she admired her son's loyalty to his team.

"Tell you what. I'll buy you lunch — just you and me. And maybe we can find a baseball card store there. I'll buy you something, within reason of course. If we get out of here by ten, we'll be home by three."

Joey reluctantly agreed. It wasn't what he had planned for the day, but he actually liked spending some one-on-one time with his mom. Because he was the oldest, he felt a sense of responsibility as the "man of the house." Whenever they did things together besides the normal everyday stuff, he always felt better afterwards. This could be one of those days. And besides, he was looking for a Red Sox team photo. He could kill two birds with one stone.

"OK. I'll go."

"Maybe you can get some ideas for your history project. St. Augustine is considered local. I bet if you walk around the historic district, something will come to you."

"Yeah, as long as it's not a ghost."

They both laughed and went back to reading their sections of the newspaper. Jennifer grabbed the scissors to clip some coupons, while Joey examined the baseball scores. Both of them had subtle smiles on their faces. It was Saturday, and life was good.

16

Chapter 4
Old Maps, Books and Photographs

Joey and his mother were in the van and heading to St. Augustine by 10:15. They had delivered Katy to her friend's house and the Lees had picked up Bobby. After the usual "mind your manners" to Katy, and "don't forget your sunscreen" to Bobby, they were off for the day's adventure.

"Sometimes I feel like we don't do enough things together," Jennifer said as they turned south onto U.S. Highway 1. "Everybody's going in a different direction. When I was growing up, families did things together."

"Times change. Besides we all have different interests."

"I know, but still, we should be spending more time together. Family is family and that hasn't changed. Maybe one of these days we should all go fishing together."

"Right," he said sarcastically. "Katy would hate that. You know how she is about bugs and slimy things."

"Yeah, but it would do her good to be around it once in a while. Sometimes I think I'm too protective."

"Mom, you're fine. She's only five. And besides, we do lots of things together. Remember last year when Aunt Mary was here and we cooked hot dogs on the beach? That was cool! Grandma and Grandpa were there, and we had a contest to see who could find the prettiest shell."

"I thought you thought that was dumb."

"Yeah it was, but Katy got so excited. Remember, we even played a game of kickball and Grandpa got Bobby out. Now that was historic!"

They both chuckled, remembering how shocked Bobby was when he felt the thump of the beach ball on his leg just before he crossed home plate. He kicked the sand and said a dirty word under his breath, but then started laughing with everyone else as Grandpa did a silly dance on the pitcher's mound.

"We ought to do that again," Joey said. "Make it an

annual event. This year would be the Second Annual Johnson Family Picnic. We could create our own history."

Jennifer smiled. They were both quiet for the next ten miles, thinking about good times and memories and family.

Soon they passed the two large conquistador statues on each side of the highway just north of St. Augustine. One had his sword pointed and looked ready to fight. Katy had always been afraid of them, and sometimes hid her face when they drove by.

Jennifer turned where a large sign proclaimed

"Welcome to St. Augustine. Founded 1565." Joey had never paid much attention to the dates before, but now he remembered from history class that the English settlers reached Jamestown sometime in the 1600s. That meant that St. Augustine was older than Jamestown.

As they drove down San Marco Avenue, they passed restaurants, motels, antique shops, and tourist stops for sightseeing tours through "The Oldest City."

Jennifer asked Joey to check the address she had written on a piece of paper. It was a family tradition that whoever sat on the passenger side was the navigator. Joey had a good sense of direction, but St. Augustine was a bit of a challenge. Many of the streets were narrow and there were usually swarms of tourists everywhere.

They stopped at the visitor information center near the old fort to get some brochures and maps. Jennifer thought they might help Joey with his history project.

Jennifer had an appointment at the St. Augustine Historical Society. As they drove past the Castillo de San Marcos, the large gray fort that had been there for more than 300 years, they saw waves of tourists streaming toward the fortress. Dozens of boats were anchored in Matanzas Bay, and American flags waved briskly on the Bridge of Lions.

"I love that old bridge," Jennifer said. "They're talking about tearing it down because they say it's not structurally sound, but I hope they never do that."

"Well, if it's a safety hazard, they need to do something about it."

"Yes, but I'd rather they fix it than destroy it. That's what my story is about. Old things, old homes that have been preserved, and how their ancient designs are still popular today."

"Sounds boring to me, but if people want to read about that, then I'm glad you're the one who's writing it. Hey, you could jazz it up with a ghost story."

"They say there are ghosts in St. Augustine. Maybe one of these days all of us can go on a ghost tour. That might be a lot of fun."

"Yeah, but it would scare Katy to death," Joey said.

"Maybe you're right. We'll wait till she's older. Besides, I thought you didn't believe in ghosts," she teased.

21

"I don't, but lots of other people do."

They turned right on Cathedral Place and drove past the statue of Ponce de Leon. The Old Market town square stretched for several blocks down to the old Government House Museum. As they approached Cordova Street, they could see the medieval-looking towers of Flagler College ahead of them.

"That's a strange building! It looks like something out of a fairy tale. Are you going to write about that?"

"No, I'm doing a story on smaller structures, like houses. But that might make a good history project for you."

"I can't get excited about an old building, Mom. If I've got to do this stupid project, I'd like it to be about people."

He was beginning to think this was a mistake. *What could possibly be interesting in this old town*, he thought.

They turned left on King Street. Joey studied the map to find a route to the St. Augustine Historical Society and Research Library.

"Oops, turn right through this big old gate," he said.

There was a huge wooden structure that went over the road. It was made of heavy beams supported by two large towers of coquina blocks with a sign that read "8 foot clearance." When they passed under it, it was like entering into another time and place. It looked like a movie set.

They were on Aviles Street, a one-way, bumpy brick road. Soon they crossed Artillery Lane where the Segui-Kirby Smith House stood. The St. Augustine Historical Society and Research Library was housed in this three-story structure that had once served as St. Augustine's first public library. There were no parking spaces in sight, but they found one a few blocks away.

They walked down Charlotte Street, and Jennifer described some of the characteristics of the old build-ings, most of which had once been homes. She pointed to the second-floor balconies that faced the east so they could catch the breezes from the bay. She talked about the entrances that opened from the sides of the homes, usually from a courtyard. With a sweeping gesture of her hands she showed him the colorful flags that hung on the balconies. Many of the buildings had tropical plants in their gardens and vines crawling up the tabby walls.

"You're going to write a great story, Mom. You really know what you're talking about. And you truly care about all this."

"That's what makes a good story. You need to find something that grabs your interest. If you do that with your project, it'll be great too."

She threw her arm around his shoulder as they walked along the uneven street. She handed him a map from the visitor's center and pointed out where they were.

"Come inside with me so I can find out how long this will take. Then you can do some exploring of your own. We can meet for lunch and check out a few shops," she suggested.

"Sounds like a plan."

They found the Segui-Kirby Smith House and entered through the courtyard. There were signs with directions to the library on the second floor.

They climbed the stairs and entered the narrow hallway that led to the receptionist's desk. While Jennifer signed her name in the guest book, Joey wandered into the library. The reading room had a large wooden table in the center. A young woman flipped through an old book and made notes in a spiral notebook. There were bookshelves around the perimeter of the room, old pictures on the walls, and a few display cases with artifacts in them.

Joey noticed a separate room labeled "Photo Collection" where file cabinets lined the walls. It was quiet, even though there were about eight people looking through books and examining papers. Usually places like this would seem boring to Joey, even creepy. But here he only felt curious. It was almost like the photographs and old leather-bound albums called out to him, trying to share their stories. *But that is ridiculous,* he thought. *What could possibly be of interest to me here?*

He had no idea that soon this place would become very special to him.

Chapter 5
This Old House

Joey didn't like these weird feelings he was having. He decided it was time to get out of there. *Things will be more normal outside,* he thought. Agreeing to meet his mother in about an hour, he left the library and walked back out into the sunshine. He didn't know which way to go, so he just wandered.

He was surprised how empty the streets were here compared to St. George Street on the other side of the square. Over there, hordes of tourists swarmed in and out of the shops and restaurants. St. Augustine was a traditional stop for many visitors on their way to Disney World in Orlando.

Except for a few bird calls and the clip clopping of horses' hooves from the tourist carriages, it was surprisingly quiet. An occasional couple walked by, probably guests at one of the bed and breakfasts near there.

He came across a construction crew restoring an old building. He remembered from his mother's descriptions that the city had restrictions on all the restoration of these buildings. He never understood why this seemed so important to some people, but watching these men work so carefully in such small spaces made him see the structures with a new respect. *I bet Grandpa would love to get his hands on one of these houses,* he thought.

He ended up back on Aviles Street in front of the Ximenez-Fatio House. A sign on the gate said it was listed in the National Register of Historic Places and they offered guided tours. Maybe he'd take the tour someday. Another sign said it was built "circa 1798," that meant around 1798. Why didn't they just say "around"?

The house had a large courtyard to the side, just like his mother had pointed out to him earlier. It also had a balcony on the second floor and was painted white to reflect the heat during steamy summer months. He couldn't imagine living in Florida without air conditioning. *Those early pioneers had to be crazy,* he thought. *Why would*

XIMENEZ-FATIO
HOUSE
CIRCA 1798

◨

Property of the National
Society of the Colonial
Dames of America in the
State of Florida

◨

Listed in the National
Register of Historic Places

they choose to live here back then?

He walked over to the open gate leading to the court-yard and peeked in. The grass was well-manicured and there were bunches of flowers growing all along the wall that bordered the yard. Several large trees provided welcome shade from the Florida sun.

Just as he turned to leave, a voice startled him.

"May I help you?" asked a thin man dressed in a colonial outfit. Joey thought he looked like Ichabod Crane.

"No, I was just looking around," he said. He tried to act nonchalant.

"Would you like to take a tour? We're going to start one in about ten minutes," the man said.

"No, I don't think so. Maybe another time. But thanks."

"I bet you'd find it interesting," the man said with an emphasis on the word "you".

Why would he think I'd find this interesting? Joey thought. *Do I look like someone who gets his jollies by touring old houses? Besides, grown men who dress up in costumes like this have to be a little silly.* As he thought of these things, he felt a little guilty. He remembered that his grandfather was a history buff. He could actually see his grandfather here in a goofy costume, telling people all about this place. A little embarrassed and ashamed of himself, he turned to leave. *So much for feeling more comfortable outside,* he thought.

Just as he started to exit the wooden gate, a family wandered in. They were obviously tourists because they all had pale white skin. *Probably from New York,* he thought. The father wore black socks with sneakers — a dead giveaway. He and Bobby had a private joke about people who dressed like that. "Yankees," they would mouth to each other. In Florida, you saw a lot of them in the summertime.

As nerdy as this family looked, it was obvious they were having a good time together. Joey watched them explore the courtyard and heard their *oohs* and *ahhs* as they examined the tropical flowers. This is what his mother was talking about earlier — doing things together, as a family. He thought about the times when his whole family, including his dad, had gone somewhere together. His parents had divorced three years earlier and his dad had moved to another city. He didn't mind admitting that he was a little jealous of this strange-looking group. And then he saw her.

She was about his age. She had shoulder-length blond hair, sparkling blue eyes, and a drop-dead gorgeous smile that she flashed at him as she walked by. *Cheerleader,* he thought. *Was it possible that those frumpy, middle-aged adults could have created this wonderful creature?*

The tour guide welcomed them, just as he had greeted Joey, and asked if they were interested in a tour. The father responded enthusiastically while the mother walked over to examine some plants.

"Is this an orange tree?" she asked.

"Yes, it is," said a pudgy woman dressed in a long skirt and apron. "The early settlers planted fruit trees in their yards. There were many times when they were not able to get food or supplies from the outside, so they had to depend on what they could grow here."

"Girls, come look at this," the mother squealed. "Let me take your picture in front of it. This is something you can share at school when you get back, Laurie."

Laurie, who was about six, joined her mother. But the teenage daughter held back. She looked at Joey who was standing there watching them and said, "Don't you just hate family vacations?"

He couldn't believe she had spoken to him. And for some reason, he didn't have a clue what she had just said, but he knew she was talking to him.

"Eh, what did you say?" he asked.

"I said, I hate family vacations."

"Oh yeah. I know what you mean. I'm down here with my mom who's working on a magazine article, and I was lucky to be able to escape for an hour."

The minute he said that, he felt guilty again. Why was he being so negative? He didn't resent his mother. The cheerleader walked toward him.

"If you're trying to kill some time, why don't you join us on the tour? It would make it a whole lot more bearable for me."

He couldn't believe his ears. She practically asked him on a date. He didn't know what to say. His mind raced. Hadn't he already decided that he would take the tour someday? Wasn't there a chance he might get some good ideas for his history project? He rationalized all the reasons why he should take the tour, but deep down inside he knew there was really only one reason why he finally agreed. And she was smiling at him.

"Come on, it'll be fun. I'm Barby Mason. What's your name?'

"Joey. Joey Johnson," he mumbled. After he recovered his composure, he said, "I bet you get a lot of comments about your name."

"Yes, I do. And if you say I look like a *Barbie* doll, I'll kick you. I get so sick of people saying that. Besides, I spell my name with a "y" instead of an "ie.""

Her younger sister overheard their conversation and added, "You don't want Barby to kick you. She's the leading scorer on her soccer team."

"You play soccer?" he asked in amazement.

"Yeah. You got a problem with that?"

"No, not at all. That's cool. I guess I just figured you were the cheerleader type."

"Well, you figured wrong."

I guess Grandma was right. You can't judge a book by its cover, he thought. She did look like a doll though. But there was no way he was EVER going to say that to her.

They joined the rest of her family outside one of the rooms on the ground floor of the house. The lady who had been discussing the fruit trees in the garden was starting the tour. She told them about building materials, antique furniture, tropical weather, the people who used to live in the house, and many other things that Joey didn't hear. Oh, he heard her voice all right, but he didn't really listen to what she said.

Barby kept pointing to things she found interesting as they walked through the rooms. There was a strange contraption made of wood and heavy fabric suspended above the table in the dining room.

"Look at this. It says here that this was used to keep the bugs away from the food. When the rope was pulled, it went back and forth and circulated the air over the diners' heads. Ingenious," she said.

Upstairs they saw several bedrooms. Most of the beds

35

had a gauze-like fabric over them, protecting the people from insects as they slept. The guide said that the beds were often moved next to the windows at night so people could be closer to any breeze that might be stirring.

"How did they stand this heat?" she whispered to Joey.

"I don't know. I was thinking about that myself. I can hardly stand it sometimes in the summer."

"Do you live here?" she asked.

"Not in St. Augustine. I live in Jacksonville just up the road, but we come here a lot."

"How cool." She giggled. "Well, not really cool, but you know what I mean."

"Yeah, I know."

The guide took them downstairs to the kitchen that was in a separate building. Joey tried to think of something intelligent to say, but nothing came to mind. He started to comment on the fireplace in the kitchen when Barby moved closer to him.

"I love seeing old places like this. It makes history come alive," she whispered in his ear. "You're so lucky to live here."

Yeah, he thought. *Today I am lucky.*

He might have to rethink this whole history thing.

Chapter 6
The Lucky One

They were standing outside of the kitchen while the tour guide posed for a picture with Barby's sister when Joey saw his mother peeking in the gate.

"Hey, Mom. I'm over here."

Jennifer waved and strolled into the courtyard. She walked to the main house.

"I just took the tour. This place is kind of cool."

Jennifer gave him a puzzled look. She wondered if this was the same young man who just an hour earlier thought there would be nothing of interest here.

Joey looked around to make sure the Masons had not left yet. They were posing for a family picture near a bright red hibiscus bush.

"Joey, come get in the picture with us," Barby called.

Joey blushed and glanced at his mom. She noticed his

embarrassment, but knew better than to say anything.

"Looks like you've made some friends," she said.

"Yeah, they were on the tour with me." He mumbled that he'd be right back and loped off across the yard.

Jennifer noticed that he brushed his hair across his forehead like he did when he wanted to look his best. He stood next to the cute blond girl and gave a fake smile. Lucky for him, the lady who was taking the picture announced that she was going to take another one because she thought she had moved the camera. This time, Joey's smile was more genuine.

Jennifer turned her attention to the house, and Joey said his goodbyes to the Masons. Barby and Joey exchanged e-mail addresses and promised to write.

"I'll send you a copy of the picture if it turns out OK," she said.

"That would be cool. I hope you'll write to me too. I'd like to know how your soccer season goes."

"Really? Do you play soccer?"

"Not any more. I used to. Now I'm into baseball."

"Cool. We live about an hour from Boston, so we go

to Fenway Park at least once a year for a Red Sox game. Do you like the BoSox?"

"Are you kidding? They're my favorite team. I have three Red Sox T-shirts and a poster of Fenway Park on my bedroom wall. This is incredible!"

After a brief silence, he said, "You're the lucky one — living an hour away from Boston. I'd give anything to live there."

She laughed. "You want to live near Boston, and I'd love to live in Florida near the beach. Isn't life strange?"

"Yes, very!"

Barby's parents walked toward the gate.

"C'mon Barby. We need to get moving if we're going to get to Orlando tonight," her father said. "Say goodbye to your friend."

"I gotta go. I'll e-mail you as soon as I get home. Bye." And she was gone.

He wondered if it really happened. A real babe, who wasn't a cheerleader, who appreciated the Red Sox, and she wanted his e-mail address. Did it get any better than this?

Maybe this trip to St. Augustine wasn't such a waste after all.

42

Chapter 7
Voices in the Garden

Jennifer had become interested in the second floor of the Ximenez-Fatio House. The two guides explained something to her with animated arm gestures. Joey was glad to have some time alone. He called to his mother that he'd be right outside and that she could take her time.

He walked down Aviles Street in the general direction of where they'd left the car. He passed a walled courtyard where he heard the voices of youngsters on the other side.

"I bet I can catch a huge fish with this pole," said one of the boys. "My father had one of his workers make it for me out of some bamboo they cut down at the plantation."

"You're lucky. All my father ever brings home is fruit,"

said the other boy.

"I bet I can hit that washtub over there under the tree," the first boy said.

There was a long pause, and then laughter.

"All you caught was a stick. Here, let me try."

After a few minutes, he heard the sound of running footsteps and more laughter. "It's a good thing there wasn't a hook on it. Mum would kill me if I had hooked those bed linens she's airing on the wall."

Joey automatically looked up at the wall, but did not see any bed linens there. He remembered how his Grandma liked to hang sheets on the clothesline instead of putting them in the dryer so they'd have that fresh-air smell. That was one of his favorite memories of spending the night at his grandparents' house. The sheets always smelled so fresh.

Joey's thoughts were interrupted when the first boy said, "Would you like to go fishing with me this after-noon?"

"Sure, but my mother won't let me. She's afraid I'll get hurt."

"Well, she doesn't have to know. We can go down beyond the barracks. There are trees near the water and we can hide if someone comes by. She'll never know."

They were silent for a moment. "Can we cook it if we catch something? I've never cooked my own fish."

"Of course, we can. We'll fix a hiding place and hide a frying pan there. I'll borrow one from the kitchen when Sadie isn't looking."

After another long pause he said, "This will be great fun! And it will be our secret place. No one else will know about it."

Their voices trailed off as they moved to another part of the yard.

Joey laughed. He and Bobby had had a similar conversation just last summer. They had found a good fishing spot in one of the neighborhood ponds, but they knew their mother would not approve of them being near water unsupervised. So they hid one of their old fishing poles in the bushes near the pond. That way, they would not have to get a pole from the garage when they wanted to go there.

Their plan worked until one day Bobby stepped in the water when he tried to catch a turtle. He got his shoes wet and muddy. Lucky for them, their mom's van was not in the driveway when they got home, so they simply hid the shoes behind a bucket of baseballs in the garage. When they looked for them a week later, they were crusted in dirt that felt like cement and smelled like the school locker room.

Joey smiled as he remembered how hard they had laughed when they found the no-longer-useable shoes. They knew they could get into trouble, but somehow it didn't matter. They weren't proud about deceiving their mom, but things were always more fun when there was some risk involved. "No guts, no glory," Bobby would say. And he was right. They privately laughed about his shoes every time someone mentioned going fishing.

The more Joey thought about it, the more he wanted to see these kids for himself. They sounded like they were about Bobby's age. He walked to the end of the block, hoping to find a gate he could peer through. But he didn't find a gate. In fact, the wall only continued for a short distance and then ended abruptly.

There was underbrush and foliage growing around a huge oak tree that had to be part of the house's property. But as he walked farther around the block, he discovered that there was no house. At least, not one that was still being used.

There was an abandoned building that looked like it had once been a house. Part of the roof had caved in on the second story and the stairs leading up to the porch were full of holes. There was no glass in the window-panes and from the looks of the weathered wood, it had not seen paint in many years.

Joey was confused. There were no other houses near this one. The undergrowth was so thick behind the structure that he knew the boys he had heard could not have been back there. He looked up and down the street, thinking maybe he'd see them walking toward the bay, but the streets were deserted except for a black cat crossing the street a block away.

There had to be an explanation. Perhaps the boys' voices had carried from another yard. But that still wouldn't explain the snapping of twigs and the thud on the washtub that he had heard. Those sounds don't carry like voices do. And what about the bed linens on the wall? He figured he simply had to find a wall with some laundry and he'd solve the mystery.

But there weren't any other houses on that block. And there was no sign of the boys, or the linens, or a washtub. There was a house, but it was obvious no one had lived in it for a long time.

As he studied the rickety structure, his mom joined him. Joey looked at her and said, "How old do you think this house is?"

"I don't know, but we could find out. The courthouse has the property records. Or maybe we could get online and see who owns it."

They stood there a moment longer. Joey felt a strange connection to this house. It once had a life, and for some reason that he couldn't explain, it seemed to be drawing him in. Maybe there were ghosts here and they were invading his brain. Maybe hunger had set in and it was affecting his mental abilities.

"Let's get some lunch," he said with a sigh. "I need some food."

"How about a cheeseburger? Maybe that will bring you back to the twenty-first century."

"Sounds good to me. Let's find some place that's air-conditioned."

Chapter 8
Houses and People

After they got home, Joey watched the Red Sox game but couldn't seem to focus on baseball. He logged on to his computer and checked out some websites about St. Augustine. He wanted to know more about the people who had lived there for the past 400 years. He told himself that all this research might prove helpful for his history project, but in reality, he was just plain curious.

His initial search found mostly information on tourism and business. He found one site that gave virtual tours of the city. He could see sailboats anchored in Matanzas Bay, and even found a 1910 photograph of the Ponce de Leon Hotel built by Henry Flagler for wealthy tourists. It looked the same today, although now it was a college instead of a hotel.

Eventually, he found some historical information

about the early Spanish settlers in St. Augustine and the French settlement of Fort Caroline to the north along the St. Johns River. He had not known the British had occupied St. Augustine for more than 20 years in the 1700s.

What he really wanted to know was what it was like to live there during the colonial days. And he especially wanted to know about that old house.

He knew he'd probably have to go back to the historical society's research library to get that kind of information. He clicked on a link to "the oldest house;" at least that's what they called it. Its official name was the Gonzalez-Alvarez House. He remembered seeing signs for it when they had been looking for a place to park.

The website had pictures of the house and some information about the people who had actually lived there. Finally! He learned that the house had been continuously occupied since the 1600s. *Now that's a historical neighborhood,* he thought.

He had just started reading about the Gonzalez, Peavett and Alvarez families when he heard the back door open and knew that his family had returned. Bobby was sunburned, smelly, and starving. Katy had fallen asleep in the van on the way home and was very cranky. Jennifer hollered to Joey for help. He logged off of the computer and went to unload the groceries from the van.

"How'd the Red Sox do?" she asked.

"Aw, OK. It was a one-to-nothing ball game . . . kind of boring."

Jennifer raised an eyebrow. "I've never heard you call baseball boring before. Are you feeling OK?"

Just then, Bobby burst into the kitchen. "Of course, he's not OK. He's a geek!" He rummaged through one of the grocery bags. "Where's the good stuff?"

"Do you mean the cabbage and broccoli?" Jennifer teased.

"No. The potato chips and cookies."

"I just put some granola bars in the pantry. You may have one, but only one. We're having barbecued chicken tonight. Does that meet with your approval?"

"I can handle that. What's for dessert?"

"Apple crisp. And if you don't get out of my way so I

can make it, there won't be any. I've invited your grandparents for dinner, so go get cleaned up before they arrive. You smell like fish. As soon as they get here, we'll fire up the grill."

She asked Joey to finish putting away the groceries and empty the dishwasher so she could start peeling apples. Katy wandered into the kitchen wearing a silver tiara she had gotten at the birthday party. The sour expression on her face made it clear that she was still not happy.

"May I have something to drink, please?" she demanded in a prissy tone.

"What would your royal highness like?" replied Joey. He made a dramatic bow.

She stared at him for a moment, trying to decide if she wanted to play along. Her face cracked slightly with an almost-smile. "I think I'd like some French champagne."

"Would you like that with a tiny umbrella, your majesty?" Joey asked.

"No, but I'd like extra bubbles," she said seriously and walked on her tiptoes over to the kitchen table.

"Please, allow me," Joey said. He scrambled behind

her and pulled the chair out for her to sit on. "Would that be pink champagne, Mademoiselle?"

"Yes, very pink, thank you."

Joey bowed from the waist, clicked his heels, and saluted her. He went to the china cabinet in the dining room and found a wine glass and a silver tray. He poured some pink lemonade into the glass, placed the glass on the tray, put a dishtowel over his left arm, and presented the glass to Katy on the tray.

She giggled as he approached. She lifted the glass from the tray with her pinky finger extended, took a sip, and belched loudly. They both roared with laughter, and Joey gave her a high five.

"Way to go! That was a good one. The king would be proud!"

However, their mother was not amused. "That was not funny! You and your brother have taught her how to do that, and I don't appreciate it. She's going to do that at the wrong time one of these days, and we're all going to be embarrassed."

"Aw, Mom, chill out! It will make her a legend in her

own time when she gets to high school. All the guys will think she's really cool."

"I doubt that! But it doesn't matter."

Turning to Katy she said, "Don't do that again. It's not cute, and it's offensive."

"What's offensive?" Bobby asked as he rounded the corner.

"You're offensive," replied Joey. "You taught your sister to burp like a construction worker, and now she's in trouble."

"Way to go, Katy," was his instant reply. Then he noticed that was probably not the right thing to say.

"I think he should be banished to the dungeon!" Joey declared.

Katy stood up on the chair, started waving her arm, and shouted, "Off with his head!"

Bobby grabbed his throat, fell to the floor, and made gurgling sounds. Max knew something was up and as always, wanted to be a part of it. He barked and ran around Bobby's thrashing body.

"OK, OK, I give up!" Jennifer said shaking her head.

"Just don't do that in front of your grandmother!"

The three kids knew not to push it any further. They slipped out of the room and disappeared to other parts of the house.

A slow smile crept across Jennifer's lips as she placed the dessert in the oven.

Chapter 9
"Nothing, Dear."

Bobby speared another drumstick as Katy crawled into her grandfather's lap at the end of dinner that night. Their stomachs were full and they were beginning to wilt — all except for Bobby.

"Where are you putting all that food, young man?" his grandmother asked.

"He's a growing boy, Bertha," replied his grandfather. "Leave him alone."

"This is the best barbecued chicken I ever ate," Bobby exclaimed. "I'm going to call it the Johnson Family Super Duper Chicken Recipe. I'm going to sell it and make millions of dollars and buy my own professional baseball team." He added more barbecue sauce to his drumstick.

"That's dumb," said Katy. "If you had millions of dollars, you could build a hospital or homes for homeless people or an animal shelter."

"An animal shelter?" asked Joey. "Why an animal shelter?"

"Because everyone always talks about helping poor people and sick people, but what about all the homeless and sick animals? You never hear anything about that, do you?"

They looked at her in amazement. She sometimes surprised them with her ideas. Grandma reached over and patted her on the arm. "That's very thoughtful, dear."

Bobby set down his chicken and said, "OK. I'll build a Super Duper Animal Shelter, right next door to the Super Duper Hospital, and when all of the people check out of the hospital, we'll give 'em a dog to take home. They'll be so thankful for being cured that they won't be upset about the dog."

The adults laughed, but Katy thought about it seriously.

"There would have to be rules, of course. You can't give a dog to just anybody. We'd have to do a background check." She thought a little more and said, "And some people might want a cat."

Everyone nodded in agreement. Even Max seemed to know that animals were being discussed. He scurried under the table and plopped down on Jennifer's foot. Grandma stood up and cleared some dishes from the table.

"How was the trip to St. Augustine today?" Grandpa inquired. "Did you get any ideas for your history project?"

"Yeah, but I'm not sure exactly what," Joey answered. "I'd still like to do something about people. Mostly there's information on buildings and stuff. I'd rather do something on how they lived, but not the same old stuff like how they cooked and how they built their houses."

"Joey toured one of the old houses while I was meeting with Mr. Corn," Jennifer said. Joey hoped that she didn't bring up the fact he had met a girl there. He didn't feel like enduring any teasing. But she didn't mention it, and he was thankful for that.

"Well, what did you think?" his grandfather asked.

"It was interesting. I don't understand how they lived without air-conditioning back then. They had to be miserable. And I'd like to know more about the everyday stuff."

He was quiet for a moment. He tried to decide whether to go on. *Oh, what the heck,* he thought.

"I found another house that was very old, too. But it was abandoned. It's the strangest thing. I could have sworn I heard kids' voices coming from the back yard. But when I went around the corner to see, there was no one there."

Grandma dropped the silverware she was clearing from the table and fumbled with it as she tried to pick it up. She gave a long serious look toward her husband, and then one to Jennifer. Joey noticed this and for some reason the hair on the back of his neck stood up.

"What?" he asked. He looked from grandparent to grandparent.

"Oh, nothing dear," his grandmother said much too quickly. "My arthritis is bothering me today." She gathered more dishes and asked if anyone was ready for dessert.

Jennifer sat there for a minute lost in thought, and then got up and started the coffee maker.

"I want extra whipping cream on mine," Bobby said. "I'm going to make it a Super Duper Apple Crisp Delight. I'll sell the recipe to a famous restaurant chain and make my second million."

Everything was normal again. Perhaps he had imagined it. What was it about that house and those voices that seemed to make his nerves react in a weird way? And why did it seem to have the same effect on the adults in his family?

No, he wasn't imagining it. But now was not the time to pursue it. If there was one thing he had learned about adults and asking them questions, it was that timing was important. He'd wait until the right time to bring it up again. He hoped that time would be soon.

Chapter 10
The Storm Brews

The next week went by quickly for Joey. It was obvious that the Red Sox were not going to make it to the playoffs, but the Yankees probably would. He avoided Jeremiah whenever possible. Sometimes their paths would cross between classes and Jeremiah would tip his cap at Joey.

Joey got the message. He knew he deserved every bit of the teasing he got. As his grandfather often said, "If you're going to dish it out, you've got to be able to take it." He didn't like it. But he did like Jeremiah, so that made it a little easier.

He aced a test in math, and got a B+ on an essay in English. When Mr. Davis asked the students to write a paragraph describing their history projects, Joey was stumped. He wrote something about St. Augustine and the people who had lived there, but he still wasn't sure exactly what he would do for his project.

He decided to check out some books on St. Augustine from the library so he could put something on his bibliography cards. The school library didn't have much so he asked his mother to take him to the public library.

After school on Thursday she dropped him off at the library nearest their house while she went to the grocery store.

"We've got a hurricane brewing, so I'm going to pick up some supplies before the stores get too crowded," she said. "It's still way out in the Caribbean, but we could start feeling it by Sunday. See you in about an hour."

Joey used the online catalog and found a few books that looked promising. He went to the history section and was glad to see that several of them were available. One book included selections written by people who lived in Florida, many of them college professors who were probably still alive. It occurred to him that he could possibly interview one of these people. That could really get him some bonus points with Mr. Davis. He'd talk to his mother about that. She could help him set it up. She was good at that sort of thing.

When he got home, he logged on to his computer to see if he had received any new e-mail. No such luck. He would probably never hear from her.

He had sent Barby an e-mail on Sunday. It took him an hour to get it just right, and he still wasn't sure it was perfect. He wasn't going to send it, but then he could hear Bobby saying, "No guts, no glory," so he pushed the "Send" button.

That had been five days ago. Maybe they were still in Florida. Who came to Florida in late summer anyway? It's so hot! And what about school? Of course, some schools didn't start until later. Or maybe they were just one of those flaky families that did as they pleased. It didn't matter. *I don't care if I hear from her,* he pretended. *I'll probably never see her again anyway.*

He read parts of some of the books he had checked out and put post-it notes on pages that he wanted to mark.

"Hey Mom, what do you think about me interviewing

one of the writers in this book?" he asked later that evening. "I think he teaches here at the university."

"That's a good idea. I'd be glad to help. By the way, I've got to go to St. Augustine again. I could wait until Saturday if you'd like to go with me."

"Sure. I want to go to the research library and find out about that house."

He was surprised at how excited he was about the prospect of going back.

On Saturday they woke up early and drove the twenty-plus miles to St. Augustine. Bobby spent the night with a friend, but Katy was with them this time. As the sun peeked over the treetops on the east side of the highway, Katy sang, "The sun will come out tomorrow . . . "

Jennifer glanced at Joey, and they exchanged smiles. Katy loved watching movies and she especially liked musicals. She knew all of the words to the songs of her favorite ones. She would memorize some of the lines from the movies and would often repeat them when it was appropriate in real-life situations. Joey figured Katy would grow up to be a writer or movie producer some day. Some of his friends had little sisters who were real pains. Katy was different. She was a keeper.

They arrived early before most of the tourists. Jennifer took Katy with her to visit a few courtyards that were to be featured in her article.

Joey went to the research library, signed in, and asked the clerk at the desk how he would find information on a particular address. He could tell the woman was a little suspicious of his motives, so he explained that he was doing a history project and showed her his student ID card. That seemed to satisfy her. After that, she was helpful.

"We have to be careful with these books," she explained. "They are very old and our job is to preserve them."

"Yes, ma'am," he said. He thought adding "ma'am" was a nice touch. Obviously she did too, because she called him "dear" after that.

He flipped through several books. He discovered that many of the early inhabitants of St. Augustine came from England, Scotland, Ireland, Germany, and Switzerland, and not just from Spain.

He read about the large Minorcan group that settled

in St. Augustine. He remembered seeing some Minorcan food on the menus of some of the St. Augustine restaurants. Now it made sense.

There were farmers as well as fishermen, sailors, ship carpenters, and merchants who depended on the sea. It took many craftsmen to provide the services needed for the growing community.

After about 45 minutes, he wanted to go back outside and walk through the streets. He knew he'd see things differently. He gathered his notebook, thanked the lady at the desk, and walked out into the humidity. The wind had increased and the trees were dropping leaves and branches everywhere.

He walked to the old house he had seen last week. He couldn't put his finger on it, but something was different. Spanish moss hung from several of the massive tree branches. Many of the branches almost touched the ground. The azalea bushes along the back fence looked ragged. He walked around the edge of the property, hoping to find something that indicated people had been there recently, but he found nothing.

He couldn't explain it, but every nerve in his body told him something strange was going on here.

Chapter 11
Cannons, Cemeteries and
Chocolate Alligators

It was almost 11:30 and he had agreed to meet his mother at the Old Market town square so they could get some lunch before it got too crowded. As he walked north on Charlotte Street, he stopped at the historical marker in the public market place. He read that in 1598, a standard system of weights and measures had been established for the protection of consumers. He had never thought of that before, but there had to be systems for all kinds of things to govern peoples' lives. Otherwise it would have been chaos.

He walked through the square past the war memorials. He wondered what other kinds of rules and regulations might be needed for a new colony; things like police and fire protection, hospitals, libraries, and schools.

73

He came back to the present when he saw his mother and sister. Katy sat on an old Civil War cannon, riding it like a horse. His mother stood near a gazebo, focusing her camera in the general direction of where Katy was playing.

"Hey, Mom," he said as he came up behind his mother.

"Hi! How'd it go?"

"Oh, pretty good. How'd it go for you?"

"It was great. I got some really good pictures that should help a lot when I write this thing. Give me just a minute. I want to get this picture and then we'll go eat."

She tried to get Katy in the foreground while focusing on the old Government House. The overcast sky and the shade of the huge oak trees created an eerie combination she hoped the camera would capture. After a few clicks, she put the camera back in its case and said, "Let's go!"

They strolled down St. George Street, thinking they might find a restaurant suitable for a five-year-old appetite.

"I want pizza," Katy announced.

"OK, let's see what we can find," Jennifer said.

They passed several souvenir shops and candy stores. Finally they found a small café that had pizza on the menu. When they finished lunch, Jennifer asked if they wanted to visit the old Huguenot cemetery that was near there. Joey replied with an immediate "Yes," but Katy's eyes grew large.

"Are there any ghosts there?" she asked.

"I don't think so," her mother answered.

"Besides, they only come out at night," Joey joked. "I'll hold your hand, just in case."

They walked through the old city gate that marked the beginning of St. George Street and crossed the street to the graveyard. Jennifer told them the cemetery was a public burying ground for Protestant pioneers. Most of the early settlers had been Catholic, she explained. The historical marker said the cemetery was started in 1821.

Joey was impressed by the dates on the tombstones.

"This one says this man was born in 1820 and died in 1879. I wonder who he was and how he died."

"I wonder how he lived. Who was his family?" Katy asked.

She spotted a small marker that was barely visible.

"I wonder if that one belongs to a baby."

"I don't know. There's no writing on it, or at least any writing that can still be read," Jennifer replied.

They walked along the short wall that surrounded the cemetery, and stopped at the wrought iron gate. A no trespassing sign warned them to keep out. The grounds were overgrown with only squirrels scampering around looking for acorns. Despite the fact it was mid-afternoon, it was dark inside the cemetery because of the huge oak and magnolia trees. The Spanish moss hanging from the limbs made it even more spooky-looking.

"I don't like it here," Katy said. "Can we go now?"

"Yeah, we'd better get going," Jennifer said. "I'd like to get a few more pictures before we head back. You can come with me, or I can meet you at the car in about half an hour."

"I'll take Katy for a walk, and we'll meet you at the car," Joey said.

They walked back down St. George Street where Jennifer offered to buy chocolate alligators at one of the candy stores.

"These are for later," she said. "They're Bobby's favorite. You can each select one."

"I want white chocolate," said Katy.

"I want milk chocolate," said Joey. "And get one of those for Bobby."

"I think I'll get one too, only mine will be dark chocolate. I love dark chocolate," she said. But both of them already knew that. That was their favorite gift to buy for her on special occasions. It was inexpensive, easy to find, and she loved it.

"I hope these don't melt before we get them home," she said.

"We can fix that." Joey grinned.

She thought about it for a minute. "Oh, all right. Just don't get it all over your clothes."

Joey and Katy walked back toward the car. They licked their chocolate alligators on a stick. Every time they passed a child under the age of ten, they caused a commotion.

"I want one of those," they heard as they walked on. Katy squeezed Joey's hand and smiled.

"Are you gloating, young lady?" he asked.

"Yes, I am!" she said with a giggle.

They crossed the town square and found a bench in a small corner park called St. Frances Park and sat in the shade. In the distance Joey could hear dogs barking and a mother calling to her kids.

"Come quickly children, the wind is getting worse," the woman shouted. "We must get to the fort before the rain starts again."

Joey jumped up and looked at the sky. The wind was blowing slightly, but there had been no rain this morning. The storm was still hundreds of miles away. And why would someone go to the fort to get out of the rain? It was blocks away. What did the woman mean?

"C'mon Katy. We're going to find out who's doing all that shouting."

Katy looked at him curiously. "What shouting?"

He stopped in his tracks and turned to look at her.

"Don't you hear that woman yelling?"

"No, I just hear some cars over that way." She pointed toward town.

"What about the dogs barking?"

"I don't hear any dogs. Are you OK?"

He didn't answer. He looked around the park, up at the trees, and then down the street.

"C'mon. Let's walk down here. There's something I want to see."

He walked briskly down St. Frances Street. It was hard for Katy to keep up with him and not drop her alligator.

"Wait up. I can't walk as fast as you."

He turned around to check on her, but kept up his frantic pace. "Just follow me. I won't lose you."

When he got to the old house, it looked the same as before. And there was still no one in sight. Where was the woman who was so scared? *This doesn't make sense,* he thought. *It just doesn't make sense.*

Chapter 12
Making Sense

"Mom, Joey's acting weird," Katy announced when they met Jennifer at the van.

"What do you mean weird?"

"Well, first he heard this dog barking, but I didn't hear any dog. Then he heard a woman screaming, but I didn't hear that either. And then he practically ran off and left me."

"You left your sister?" Jennifer inquired in a serious tone.

"No, I didn't leave her. She was right behind me the whole time. She's just slower than I am."

That seemed to satisfy his mother's concern about his capabilities as a responsible big brother, but not about his hearing abilities.

"What's this about dogs barking and women

81

screaming?"

"She wasn't screaming like she was scared. She was hollering at her kids. You know, like all mothers do," he said, and then realized that was probably not a good way of putting it.

"It's not a big thing. Dogs and mothers and kids are as normal as you and me and Max." He said it casually, but he didn't convince himself that it was at all normal.

There was more to it than that. It WAS a big thing. But he wasn't sure he wanted to talk about it any further right now. Fortunately, his mother dropped the subject, although she did look concerned about something. He hoped it wasn't him.

They rode home silently. Katy fell asleep. Jennifer stared at the road ahead. Joey didn't know what to think. Twice he had heard things, but couldn't explain them. And the voices didn't sound natural. They had a different accent.

He tried not to think about it, but it wouldn't leave him alone. When they got home, he went straight to his room. He wanted to be alone. His head raced with crazy thoughts. *Maybe I should go outside,* he thought. He put on his old shoes, got his bike out of the garage, and rode over to Cory's house.

He and Cory had been friends since third grade. Cory was washing his mother's car, but was just about finished. Joey flopped down under a pine tree and pointed out some cloudy spots on the car. He jumped up when Cory pointed the water hose in his direction.

"Hey, watch it, these are my dancing shoes," he said.

"Yeah, and I'm just trying to make you dance."

Soon they were throwing a football back and forth. They had just begun a rip-roaring game of whiffle ball when Cory's mother said they had to go to the mall.

"See you later, Twinkle Toes," he said, and disappeared into the house.

Before he went home, Joey rode his bike around the block to clear his head. But his head wouldn't clear. As soon as he was alone, it all came rushing back to him. *OK, I'm a bright kid,* he thought. *I can figure this out.*

The boy he heard last week called his mother "Mum,"

and said his dad worked on a plantation. Today the woman referred to the fort as the place they would go to in a storm. Both of them used words that sounded strange. No one talks like that, at least not now.

And then it hit him like a thunderbolt. That is the way people talked long ago, like when the early settlers were there. Didn't the British call their mothers "Mum"? He had just read about the plantations in the 1700s and about the British occupation from 1763 to 1784. Was it possible he was hearing voices from the past?

That didn't make sense. Maybe the voices were from tour guides acting out historical roles. They could be talking like people did long ago for a touch of realism for the tourists. Now that sounded logical. He felt much better now. He had an explanation. Maybe now he could get on with his life.

This history project was really beginning to annoy him!

Chapter 13
Absolutely Delightful

"Joey, we need to talk," his mother said as she came into his room later that evening.

"Sure, what about?"

"About these voices you've been hearing."

"I've been thinking about that," he said. "Don't you think it could be one of those tour groups? Maybe I was just hearing some colorful tour guides making their speeches a little more dramatic."

"Yes, that's a possibility," she agreed. She hesitated. "But there's something else that I need to share with you. It's kind of strange and we never talk about it, but now is as good a time as any to tell you."

"What is it? Is something wrong?"

"No, nothing like that. It's just that sometimes things happen that we can't explain." She paused for a while, searching for the right words.

He was getting nervous. This was like the time his parents told him they were getting a divorce. The only thing worse could be news that someone was sick. Had his grandparents been feeling OK lately? Or maybe it was his mother. Maybe she had cancer or something. His heart pounded. *Please don't let it be anything really bad*, he thought.

"Many years ago your great-grandmother's sister, that would be my Great Aunt Rosie, was sent to a special doctor because some of the family members thought she was crazy."

Oh, this is not good, he thought.

"She made people uncomfortable because she claimed she could hear voices from the past."

Jennifer paused for a minute to let it sink in. Joey sat on the bed with his legs crossed. He looked at his hands and tried to prepare for some horrible news regarding a member of his family. His head jerked up. He stared at his mother.

"What did you say?"

"Aunt Rosie heard voices." She took a deep breath. "But for what it's worth, she was not a kook. She was not crazy. In fact, I adored her."

"She claimed she could hear things that other people could not. It wasn't all the time. It just happened occasionally. No one could explain it, and many people didn't believe her. They thought she was just being dramatic or wanted attention." She paused again.

"It never did anyone any harm. The things she heard, or claimed to have heard, were not of any significance. Just everyday things, snippets of conversations from people who lived in that place many years before."

She paused again as Joey digested what she said.

"I was thinking about her last week when you mentioned what you had heard in St. Augustine."

Joey could feel the hair on the back of his neck prickle again. They were getting into that "not making sense" area, and he didn't like it.

"Are you saying I'm like her?"

"I don't know. All I know is she heard voices from the past, and now it seems you do too. If it makes you feel any better, I DO believe you heard these things and I DON'T think you are crazy."

If his mom believed in him, he knew he wasn't totally off his rocker.

"OK, so what happened to her? Please don't tell me they put her in the loony bin."

"Well, nothing really happened. Her husband was a prominent attorney who sat on the town council. He wasn't excited about Rosie's extrasensory perceptions going public. For years Rosie just didn't talk about it.

"But after Uncle Frank died and she got older, she didn't care what people thought. People found her eccentric. A few family members were embarrassed, but it all seemed so harmless that no one considered it a problem.

"She lived to the ripe old age of 92. She was a neat lady. She was interested in art, music, current events, and even sports. She loved to read. She kept a journal and wrote wonderful letters."

Joey tried to absorb it all.

"You said they took her to a doctor. Did he ever diagnose any illness?"

"No. You have to remember — this would have been in the 1950s. The doctor who examined her said there was nothing wrong with her. In fact, he said she was 'absolutely delightful.'

"The family eventually dropped the subject of her mental health. Most of them ignored her, and she became more reclusive as she got older. I think she was smart enough to know that talking about her 'hidden talents,' as she called them, only upset people. She grew tired of fighting those battles, and kept more to herself.

"I remember one summer when we visited my grandmother, Rosie asked me to help her plant some flowers in her garden. She had the most beautiful petunias. To this day when I see petunias, I think of her.

"Rosie lived in the house behind my grandparents where my mother grew up. I was very young then, maybe six or seven, and I spent several afternoons with her that summer. We picked blackberries and made tarts. She was wonderful!"

There was another long silence.

"So what am I supposed to do? Do you think I'm like Aunt Rosie? Is it possible that I am hearing voices from the past, or is there a logical explanation for all this?"

"I honestly don't know, Joey. I just thought you should know the family history. I can't explain Aunt Rosie, and I can't explain what you've heard. If you want, we could talk to some doctors about it. But to be honest with you, I'm not overly concerned. If there is such a thing as 'hidden talents' and you have them, then I think you need to be aware of it and not let it freak you out. It's just one of those things we don't fully understand. If you would like to talk to someone, I'll be with you all the way.

"Why don't you think about it and let me know if you want to pursue it. But remember, I'm always in your corner and you can talk to me anytime." She got up to leave.

"And Joey, I think you're wonderful too!" She kissed him on the top of the head and left.

Joey sat on his bed staring into space. An hour ago he had things all figured out. Now he didn't know what to think.

Chapter 14
The Unexplained

Joey had a hard time getting to sleep that night. His mind wouldn't shut off. He was tired and groggy when his mother announced it was 8:30 the next morning.

"Rise and shine everyone. Time to get ready for church," she mumbled with a piece of bagel in her mouth. "I'm making pancakes, so get moving or you won't have time to eat."

Bobby stumbled down the hallway to the bathroom and discovered Katy had beaten him to it. The door was locked and she was singing "Somewhere Over the Rainbow."

"Let me in! I gotta go," Bobby shouted and pounded on the door.

"Not by the hair of my chinny, chin, chin," came the answer.

"Then I'll huff and I'll puff and, and . . . you'll be sorry when you get out."

There was no response. In fact, there was no sound at all.

"Katy! Hurry up! I'm going to pee on the floor, and then you'll be in big trouble."

The door opened slightly. "What's the magic word?"

"Get outta my way is the magic word."

"No, sorry," and the door slammed shut.

"Mom! Katy's hogging the bathroom and I gotta go," he howled.

Jennifer peeked around the corner of the kitchen. She had a dishtowel in her right hand, and her left hand was on her hip. She looked frustrated.

"Why don't you go use my bathroom? Do you always have to yell at her?"

At that moment Katy opened the door, walked past Bobby and said, "The magic word is please. All you had to do was say please."

"As soon as I'm done in here, I'll get you," Bobby said.

Bobby reached out to grab her, but she was too fast. She bolted for Joey's room and ran giggling toward his bed. Joey threw back the covers and let her crawl in.

"Hide, I'll protect you!" Joey said.

When Bobby came out of the bathroom, he got down on all fours and crawled to Joey's room. Max knew this usually meant wrestling on the floor at some point, so he barked and nipped at Bobby's nose. Bobby made growling sounds, which made Max more excited. By the time he reached Joey's room, Katy was squealing with anticipation. When Bobby came after her like this, she usually got tickled and she didn't like that.

"Don't let him tickle me, Joey. Please!"

Joey jumped up, grabbed an old golf club they had found near their fishing hole, and started swishing it like a sword.

"I'll save you," he said.

By now Bobby was inside the room and growling even louder. Max tried to jump up on the bed, but his short legs couldn't make it. Katy squeezed a pillow in front of her and used it as a shield. Joey jumped between Bobby and the bed and pretended to stab him with the golf club. Bobby fell over and did an Academy Award-winning dying scene. He sputtered and choked and flailed his arms and legs. When he was finally still and lying sprawled on the floor, Max pounced on him and licked his face.

"Yuck! Cut it out you stupid dog." He wiped his arm across his face.

"He's not a stupid dog," Katy said. "He's alive and you're dead. So who's the stupid one?"

"Oh, are you calling me stupid?" Bobby asked. He started to get up.

"No, I just don't like it when you call Max stupid. Dogs can be very sensitive."

Bobby looked at Max and then at Joey who was now practicing his putting with the golf club.

"Now that's stupid!" he said, pointing at Joey. "He couldn't sink a putt if his life depended on it."

"Oh, yeah. This is my Super Duper Can't Miss Golf Club. It used to belong to a wizard who liked to golf. All you have to do is say the magic words and you can't miss."

"And what are the magic words?" Bobby asked.

"Please and thank you," Katy said.

"Yes, that's correct," Joey said. "Please and thank you Mr. Super Duper Putter. I'd like to win the Tournament Player's Championship Golf Tournament and make millions of dollars over the next ten years. Then I'd retire at age 23 and spend the rest of my life visiting every major league baseball stadium in the country."

"Can I go?" Katy asked.

"Certainly, and you can bring along your friend if you want." He pointed to Bobby.

"He's not my friend. He's my brother," she said.

There was total silence for a minute as they let her comment sink in. Then they all started laughing at the same time.

"I hope everyone is dressed and ready to go," Jennifer yelled from the kitchen. She knew they weren't, and they knew she knew they weren't.

"The bus leaves in twenty minutes," she said. She always said that when they were getting ready to go somewhere. In ten more minutes she'd say, "The bus is leaving in ten minutes." And then she would finally say, "The bus is leaving." And she would leave.

They were used to this. And the funny thing was, it worked. Once when Bobby was dawdling in the bathroom fussing with his hair, she gave him two minutes to get in the car. He didn't make it in time and had to run after the car as she backed out of the driveway. He wasn't sure if she would have left him, but he wasn't going to take that chance again.

One by one they scurried to the kitchen in their Sunday clothes. That meant the boys had to wear a shirt with a collar and Katy wore a dress. Their mother insisted that they look nice when they went to church.

While they ate their pancakes, Bobby asked Joey which major league baseball park was his favorite.

"If you had a million dollars, which stadium would you visit first?"

"I know the answer to that one," Katy said.

"OK smarty, which one?" Bobby said.

"Fenway Park in Boston," she replied with a smug look on her face.

"That's right, how did you know that?" Joey asked.

"It's not rocket science, you know. You're a huge Red Sox fan, so of course it would be Fenway."

"But what about Wrigley Field?" Bobby asked. "That's one of the most famous baseball stadiums in the whole world."

"Yeah, I'd like to go there too," he said dreamily. "But I'd have to go to Boston first."

They talked as they ate their breakfast. Katy dribbled syrup on the tablecloth, and Bobby sloshed chocolate milk on his shirt. He figured no one would notice because it was a dark shirt.

They got into the van, and Bobby and Joey sat in the back seat and gave Katy the front.

"Do you think there's such things as wizards?" Bobby asked Joey.

Joey looked at him like he was crazy. Remembering his conversation with his mother the night before, he said, "I don't know Bobby. There are a lot of things we can't explain."

They rode the rest of the way to church in silence.

Chapter 15
Scholarly Advice

Later that week, Joey used the Internet to find the phone number of a college professor who was one of the writers of a book he had checked out of the library. He asked his mother if she'd call for him.

"You need to call him," she said.

"Naw, he won't want to talk to a kid."

"I think you'd be surprised. If you explain you're working on a history project for school and tell him exactly what you're trying to find, I bet he'd be glad to help you."

He made a list of questions. He asked his mother to stay near him while he called, so on the remote chance that this guy was willing to meet with him, he could schedule an appointment when she could drive him there. He also wanted her close for encouragement.

He dialed the number and got a secretary who said

Dr. Roberts was in class at the moment, but he should be back in his office in about an hour. Joey said he would call back then.

It was a long hour. He got more nervous. Finally, he called back. The professor answered on the third ring.

"Hello, Dr. Roberts here," a distinguished-sounding voice said.

Ho boy, Joey thought. Maybe he could just hang up. No, that wouldn't work. Maybe the guy had caller ID. Besides, his mother was standing right there. Why, for the love of baseball, did he ask her to hang around? *Oh well, here goes nothing*, he thought.

"Uh, Dr. Roberts . . . " Joey paused. "My name is Joey Johnson. I'm an 8th grader at Thomas Jefferson Middle School." He waited a moment and when there was no comment from the other end, he continued. "I'm doing a project for my history class. It's on St. Augustine, and I was wondering if I could talk to you about some things."

Oh, great. Why did I say "some things"? he thought. *That sounded so lame. I should have said some facts or in-*

*formation or some historical data, but no, I said "some things"
and sounded like a real idiot.*

He thought about hanging up and telling his mother
they got disconnected, but then he remembered he had already given his name and his school. *I AM an idiot. Whatever possessed me to do this? I HATE this history project.*

Then a response came.

"I'd be pleased to help you. What kinds of things do
you need to know?"

Oh wow. Joey's spirits soared. *I can do this*, he
thought.

"I'm trying to find out about some of the everyday ac-
tivities that happened in the early days in St. Augustine.
Like what kinds of food they ate, what they did in their
spare time, and things about their family life. What did
the kids do for fun?"

"I see," Dr. Roberts said. "Well, there are several books
that I could refer you to, and I'd be glad to answer any
specific questions." There was a short pause. "Do you
have e-mail, Joey?"

"Yes, I do."

"Why don't you give me your e-mail address and I'll send you a list of books that might be helpful. Maybe you can find them at the library or in a bookstore. If that presents a problem, then I'll be glad to lend you some of mine."

Wow, this guy is great! And Mr. Davis is going to be so impressed, he thought.

Joey gave Dr. Roberts his e-mail address.

"After you've read through these, and if you still have questions, I'd be glad to talk with you further. I'm sure you're not interested in reading all the books, but there will be some sections that should be helpful to you. You could also check with the historical library in St. Augustine, although I know that might be a little difficult to arrange."

"Oh no, not at all. In fact, I've already been there twice. My mom took me there. It's just hard to find exactly what I'm looking for."

"Oh yes, I know. Historical research isn't always easy. But it sounds like you're off to a good start. Who knows, you might become a historian yourself some day."

Fat chance, Joey thought. But he wasn't going to say that to this professor and author.

"I don't know. This is an interesting project." He didn't feel guilty for telling a lie. Because in fact, it wasn't a lie. It was actually starting to get interesting.

"Well, good. It's always good to know that young people are doing things in school that have some meaning for them."

Joey wasn't sure this had any significant meaning for him, and then he remembered the voices. He was interested in getting to the bottom of that, but he didn't think his school had anything to do with that. It didn't matter though. This professor thought it did, so why burst his bubble?

"It has been fun learning about things that happened here near where we live," he replied. *What a bunch of baloney*, he thought to himself. But at the same time, he was kind of proud of the way he came up with that response so quickly. He had never been good at telling lies.

"Well, Joey, it's been nice talking to you. I'll e-mail you a list of books and you can e-mail me if you can't find all the answers to your questions. And if you'd like to come out to the university some afternoon, just call the department secretary and set up an appointment. I have mostly morning classes except for the one today, so I could be available for you after school."

"Thanks a lot, Dr. Roberts. You've been very helpful."

"And Joey, I'd like to see a copy of your finished report. I bet it will be good," Dr. Roberts added.

Oh great, now why did he have to go and say that? Just what I need, more pressure!

"Sure, I'd be glad to," he said. But he didn't mean it. There was no way he was sending a college professor a copy of his dorky report. This guy would find it stupid. A real joke. He'd just have to tell him it got lost in the mail.

"You can e-mail it to me."

"Sure," Joey said. *So much for getting lost in the mail.* "Thanks, again. Good-bye." And he hung up. He had jumped from one mess right into another.

"You look upset. It sounded like he was helpful," his

mother said.

"Yeah, he was great. Just great! He's going to e-mail me a list of books."

"That sounds wonderful. So why the long face?"

"He wants me to send him a copy of my report when I'm finished. I can't do that, Mom. He teaches college kids. Mine will seem so childish to him."

"Oh, so that's what's got you down." She was thoughtful for a moment, because she didn't want to sound too corny.

"Joey, you're a great writer, and you've got a good subject. If it would make you feel any better, I'd be glad to proofread your paper before you turn it in. I've read many of your other reports, and they're good. Besides, there are some college kids who can't write worth a flip. Your paper could be a real treat for him."

He didn't answer, but gave her a pathetic look.

"I'm going to my room to check my e-mail," he said quietly. As he headed toward his bedroom, he realized how supportive his mother had been. She took him to St. Augustine, and drove him to the library, and stood by him while he called the history professor.

"Thanks, Mom. You've been a big help!" he shouted from the hallway.

"You're welcome, son. Just remember me when you get the Pulitzer Prize. And if there's a Nobel Prize in your future, I get ten percent of the money. You hear me, nothing less than ten percent!" she shouted back.

He grinned as he headed for the computer.

He logged on and had three new e-mails. None from the university. Bummer. But three from some baseball buddies. He didn't feel like talking baseball right now. But wait. The last one caught his eye. In the subject line it read, "BoSox rule!" He was the only one of his friends who liked the Red Sox. He didn't recognize the e-mail address in the "From" line.

Then it hit him. Could it be? His heart pounded. His hands got sweaty. His fingers could hardly work the mouse. One click on the Inbox and there she was.

"Hey, Joey. Remember me? Barby Mason. How are you?" he read.

Remember her? Was she kidding? How could he forget?

This day was beginning to turn out OK. Better than OK. Fantastic! *Isn't life strange*, he thought. *Just when you're having a really lousy day, something wonderful happens to turn everything around.*

He clicked the "Reply" button and started typing.

Chapter 16
Reading and Writing

At school the next day Joey learned a rough draft of his history project was due the following week. Why hadn't he built a stupid fort out of Popsicle sticks like one kid was doing, or made a documentary video about the the Kinglsey Plantation like some of the girls who took TV production were doing? Then he wouldn't have to write anything. *I've got the dumbest project in the class*, he thought.

When he got home from school, he found a stack of books on his bed with a note.

"I was downtown today so I went by the library and rummaged through the history section. Here are some of the books on Dr. Roberts' list. Good luck!" It was signed with a smiley face, which meant it was from his mom.

He had planned to read the new issue of *Sports*

Illustrated, but decided to find the information he needed for his history paper. Many of the books smelled musty and had yellow pages. Either they were very old, or they didn't get checked out much. He figured it was probably both.

Being old wasn't all bad if you're a history book, he decided. In fact, it kind of put him in the appropriate mood. He read about how the houses were constructed and the streets were laid out. He read about how the people learned of news by reading notices posted to a wall and how they were dependent on ships to bring them supplies and food from other places. He read about the plantations outside of town, and slavery, and occasional Indian uprisings.

Cool! They had Indian raids right here in Florida. The Wild West had nothing on us, he thought.

Their everyday lives were affected by events beyond their control — like a smallpox threat in 1780, a yellow fever epidemic in 1821, and several bad freezes that ruined all the citrus trees. Life was hard for those early settlers. And if that wasn't enough, every time a new flag was raised over St. Augustine indicating a change in authority, new leaders would be appointed from some other country across the ocean, and the lives of all the inhabitants would be affected.

It was a complicated story. The times were difficult, but Joey found it fascinating. It was amazing to him that for more than 400 years people struggled against the forces of politics and the challenges of living in a humid, semi-tropical, mosquito-infested climate — and they had survived.

He had a new respect for those people who once lived within miles of his home. They were real people with real stories. They had problems and needs and dreams — just like him and his family. They weren't just names and dates and events in a book — they were real people.

Joey turned on his computer and began to write.

Chapter 17
Boston, Beaches and Barby

It took him three evenings to finish his report. Then it took part of his weekend to get the bibliograpy together and all of his note cards organized.

"Why do teachers want to see note cards?" he complained to his mother. "Lots of kids write the cards after they write the report."

"It doesn't matter, dear. That's part of the assignment, so you have to do it."

It didn't make sense to Joey, but he knew she was right. He was relieved when he finally finished, and was pleased with the way it turned out. But at the same time, he felt a little disappointed when it was all over. He had learned a lot of new things and was even beginning to like history.

As the printer spit out his final draft, he signed online before going to bed. Bingo — there she was. Barby sent him a message. He beamed.

"Hey, Joey. What's new with you?"

"Not much. I just finished my history project on St. Augustine. What's new in Bean Town?"

Joey had been receiving e-mails from her every day. She usually wrote to him in the evening after she finished her homework. Sometimes she was online and they talked about school and what they were studying. She was a serious student and not one of those dumb, giggly girls.

"I got a bad bruise on my leg at soccer practice yesterday, so I'll have to wear jeans for the rest of the week. It's gotten cool here already, so shorts are out anyway. What's the weather like in Florida?"

"It's not as hot as it was, but it's still in the 80s. And so far we've been lucky — none of the hurricanes have hit us."

"You're sooooo lucky to live in Florida. If I lived there, I'd go to the beach every day."

He knew what he wanted to say to that, but he was

too scared to say it. *Oh well, what the heck,* he thought.

"The next time you come to Florida, I'll take you to the beach. We have a great one about fifteen minutes from my house. The sand is white and the water is a beautiful blue green," he wrote. He thought he was laying it on pretty thick, so he stopped there. Besides, he was anxious to hear her reaction.

"You're on! I plan to spend every spring break in Florida when I go to college. You can give me a tour of the most beautiful beaches. And then when you come to Boston, I'll take you to Fenway."

He could hardly believe it. She was talking about coming back to Florida and about future plans together. Maybe it would never happen, but maybe, just maybe, it would. That was enough for now.

"You've got a deal! Beaches and Boston — sounds like a great exchange."

"I gotta run. My mom freaks out on Sunday nights. She wants us to start the week off with a good night's sleep. I can hardly wait till I go to college and I can make up my own rules. Talk to you later. Bye."

"Bye," he replied, and then logged off. He wished he had a picture of her. Maybe tomorrow he'd ask her to send him the one they had taken in the garden.

He had a hard time getting to sleep that night. So much had happened in the past six weeks. He had met Barby and now they were in a relationship, even though it was happening electronically. He had discovered that history wasn't all that bad. And he learned that not everything could be explained. He still wasn't sure about the voices, but even that didn't bother him tonight.

He fell asleep thinking about beaches, Boston and Barby.

Chapter 18
School — Then and Now

Two weeks later on a Friday, Mr. Davis returned their history projects. Joey worried because he had only done a written report. Others had done a presentation or a video or something three-dimensional.

He opened the cover to his report carefully so no one else would see. He usually made good grades on tests and papers, so the other students expected him to make "A's" on everything. It was embarrassing if he didn't get an "A." And it was embarrassing if he did. He had learned a long time ago to keep his grades private.

But this time, he was proud of his work. He really wanted an "A" because he had put so much time and energy into the research. And he got it! He couldn't stop the silly grin that spread across his face.

There was a note from Mr. Davis scrawled on his

cover page. "Good report, Joey! You did a great job on the research. Your bibliography is impressive."

The rest of the classroom echoed a mixture of cheers, sighs and groans. Joey's baseball buddies were happy with the"B"they got on their History of Baseball in Florida video. He had heard all about it on the bus ride home for the past several weeks. At first he was a little jealous of the fun they had making it, but he knew if he got involved with that group he would end up doing most of the work. Besides, he was glad he picked St. Augustine as his subject.

When the bell rang, Mr. Davis motioned for Joey to come see him.

"Joey, I was impressed with the quality of the books you used for your research."

"Thanks, but I had some help."

"Yes, I know. I bumped into Dr. Roberts at a historical society meeting last week. He told me that a middle school student had called him for some information on St. Augustine. When I read your report, I knew it had to be you."

"Yeah, we talked on the phone and then he

e-mailed me a list of books to use."

"Well, that was very enterprising of you. Don't forget to send a copy of your report to Dr. Roberts. He asked me to remind you."

A frown crossed Joey's face. Mr. Davis added, "Don't worry. It's a good report. You have nothing to fear."

"Thanks," Joey mumbled. "I gotta go. I'm going to miss my bus."

He dashed past the school's library to put some books in his locker for the weekend, and thought about what school must have been like back in the pioneer days. Books and paper were scarce. There were no computer labs or even shelves full of encyclopedias.

They probably just learned basic reading, writing, and arithmetic. They didn't need much training because there were fewer professions for people to pursue back then. He remembered reading about apprenticeships where young people could learn skills from older people already established in a trade or profession. But that would limit the kinds of things a person could learn. You would be trained in only one area. That would be boring.

He was glad he lived now. He had access to computers, television, books, and air-conditioning. How did they survive without air-conditioning?

Despite all the reasons why he didn't want to live then, he was still intrigued. The people he had read about were real to him now.

When he got home from school, he asked his mother if they could visit St. Augustine during the weekend. He wanted to walk the streets again. He didn't know exactly why he felt that way; he just did. Maybe this was another one of those things that just couldn't be explained.

Chapter 19
A Long Walk to the Old Fort

His mother agreed to go to St. Augustine on Saturday after Bobby's baseball game. The game took longer than anticipated because there was a rain delay. When it was finally over, Jennifer suggested the whole family go. They could have a picnic dinner. They would stop at a drive-through at a fast food restaurant when they got there instead of taking the time to prepare something at home.

The crowds in St. Augustine were lighter than usual because of the overcast weather. They spread a blanket on the grassy area around the Castillo de San Marcos.

"Did you know there's been a fort on this location since 1672?" Joey said. "The early fort had been made of wood, but eventually it was built out of coquina which they got right over there at Anastasia Island." He pointed

123

south toward the lighthouse.

"You sure know a lot about St. Augustine, Joey," Katy said.

"Yes, I'm actually brilliant, you know," he replied. Bobby rolled his eyes and made gagging sounds.

"It's really beautiful here, isn't it?" Jennifer said. No one answered. They were all thinking different thoughts.

Joey looked toward the fort and wondered how many other people over the past 300 years had walked on those same grounds. Katy enjoyed watching the horse-drawn carriages line up along the Avenida Menendez, waiting for tourists to hire them. And Bobby threw stones into the bay.

"You'd think he'd had enough throwing for one day," his mother said. She unwrapped the burgers and chicken nuggets.

"Come and get it," she said.

After they finished eating, Katy asked if she could get a closer look at the fort. Bobby and Joey each grabbed one of her hands and raced toward the drawbridge with Katy half running and half flying, squealing with delight.

The fort was already closed for the day, but they were able to read some of the historical markers and look into the moats that surrounded the coquina structure.

"Look over there," Joey pointed to a section of the wall. "You can see where a cannon ball was fired at the fort from a ship in the bay. There's just a dent in the wall. The coquina absorbed the impact of the cannon balls. The walls didn't catch fire like wood, because they were made out of shells."

"You sound like *The History Channel*," Katy said. A few weeks ago Joey would have been insulted by that comment, but he wasn't now.

"I remember there's a dungeon inside the fort," Bobby said. "We came down here on a field trip when I was in the fourth grade. It was so cool! It's kind of dark in there, so Jason Horn and I hid around a corner and jumped out and scared a bunch of girls. You could hear them scream for miles."

"That was mean," Katy scolded. "You shouldn't do things like that."

"Yeah, I know. We got in trouble and had to go sit on

the stairs for ten minutes. It was hot as blazes, and everyone came over and laughed at us."

"Serves you right," she said.

They walked along the wall, but soon Katy grew tired.

"Let's go back and ask Mom if we can get some candy before the shops close, " Bobby suggested. "You ask her though," he said to Katy. "She'll do it for you."

They returned to the picnic blanket and Katy asked her mother about getting some chocolate.

Jennifer hesitated, and looked at Bobby disapprovingly.

"How much candy did you eat in the dugout today?" she asked.

"Aw, mom. That was hours ago. Chocolate alligators are a tradition. They're a special treat. If we really want this to be a Super Duper Day, then we have to have something special."

"And you know what Grandma says," Katy added, "You can never have enough chocolate."

"OK," Jennifer said. "You win. Chocolate alligators

for everyone!"

Joey was silent during this exchange. In fact, he had been rather quiet throughout the whole picnic.

"Mom, would you mind if I took a walk instead?" he asked.

Jennifer was slow to respond. She finished cleaning up hamburger wrappers and napkins. She gave him a sideways look, but eventually said, "OK."

"Don't go far and don't be gone long. It will be dark soon and we need to get back."

"I'm just going to walk along the water. I'll meet you at the car in about half an hour. That should give the munchkins enough time to satisfy their sugar cravings."

Both Katy and Bobby were offended by the term "munchkin."

"You think you're such a big shot," Katy said.

"Yeah, more like a big snot," Bobby snarled at his older brother.

"OK, guys," Jennifer said. "Leave him to his walk and we'll go get some candy."

"Only old farts take walks," Bobby shouted over his

shoulder just as an elderly couple was walking by. Jennifer rolled her eyes and gave Bobby a dirty look.

"What did he say?" the old man said to his wife. "Was he talking to us?"

"No dear. He said it's a long walk to the old fort." She winked at Jennifer as they passed.

"He's got that right," the old man mumbled. They continued up the path to the fort.

Jennifer and Katy and Bobby giggled as they walked toward the candy store.

Chapter 20
Adventures

Joey strolled along the promenade toward the Bridge of Lions. He could hear music coming from one of the boats anchored in Matanzas Bay. It sounded like some of the oldies music his mother listened to on the radio. He wondered when that song had been popular. It seemed like everything he saw and heard now had some kind of connection to the past. So much had changed for him in the past few weeks.

He kept thinking about the voices. Were they real? Had he imagined them? Was there a logical explanation? Or did he have some special gift like his Great-Great Aunt Rosie? Whatever it was, it had definitely changed things for him.

He saw two tourists taking a photograph by one of the large white lion statues at the entrance to the bridge.

He didn't want to be around tourists, so he reversed his path and walked back to the fort where it was much quieter. He walked along the wall that ran between the fort and the bay. When the wall came to an end, he found a path that led down to the water. The tide was up, but there were some large stones along the waterline so he was able to continue walking without getting his shoes wet. He saw several big houses along the waterfront and he hoped he wasn't trespassing.

Then he heard it. There was a voice off in the distance, mixed with the sound of splashing water. He stopped moving and cocked his head so he could hear better. It was definitely a voice, but it sounded far away. He walked a little farther and realized the voice was actually very close. Whoever it belonged to spoke in a whisper.

He moved slowly toward the voice. It came from behind a large scrubby bush at the water's edge. His palms were getting sweaty and his heart began to race.

Then a strange thing happened. A small, crudely made toy boat came bobbing in the water from behind the bush. The tide was taking it out, and the splashing sound was someone trying to pull the boat back to the shore.

Joey stared at the boat. He blinked. After a long moment, he decided he had nothing to lose by trying to retrieve it. He had to make sure it was real. He took off his shoes and threw them onto the grass behind one of the houses so they wouldn't get wet.

Just as he was about to step into the water, a small boy waded out from behind the bush.

"Hey, can you help me? My boat is getting away," the boy said.

Joey stared at the boy. His mind raced.

"Are you OK?" the boy asked after a few seconds.

"Eh, yeah," Joey answered. "Where did you come from?"

The boy hesitated. "Up there." He pointed to a trail that led to a house.

"We're visiting my grandparents, and I'm not supposed to be down by the water. Now will you help me get my boat?"

"Sure," Joey replied. He wanted to know more about this boy, but he decided if he retrieved the boat, then he could ask him more questions. The boy had a strange haircut and his clothes looked a little odd, but he was definitely real.

Joey waded out a few feet, hoping he didn't cut his feet on any oyster shells. He realized he couldn't reach the boat without getting his pants wet. He came back to shore and found a branch that looked like it would do the job. He went back into the water and stretched his arms as far as he could to reach the boat.

Just then, a woman's voice called out, "Robbie, where are you?"

"Oops," the boy said. "I better go. She'll skin me alive if she finds me near the water again."

"Wait," Joey shouted. "Don't go!"

But it was too late. The boy had scrambled up the bluff and was out of sight.

Joey wanted to follow, but decided to get the boat first. It took him three more tries with the stick before he was able to snag the small piece of wood. As soon as he got it, he waded ashore and climbed up the same trail the boy had used.

He found himself in the backyard of a two-story Victorian house. An old woman knelt near a flowerbed with her back to Joey. When she turned to grab a small shovel, she noticed him.

"May I help you?" she asked. She took off her gloves, wiped her brow with her arm, and struggled to get to her feet.

"I was looking for a little boy," he said. "To give him his boat. He just came through here. Did you see him?"

"No, can't say as I did," she answered. "But then I've had my head buried in these pansies for the past hour. And my hearing's not what it used to be."

"I got the impression he was staying here."

"You must be mistaken," she said. "It's just me and my husband here now. Sometimes kids cut through our yard to get to the water, but I don't remember seeing anyone come through today."

Joey was getting frustrated.

"I think I'll go out front and see if I can find him."

He bolted through the yard, hoping he wasn't too late. When he got to the street, he looked both ways. There was no sign of the boy. He ran halfway up the block one direction and then back the other way, but found no one. Finally he sat down on the curb and held the boat out in front of him. *At least I didn't make this up*, he thought.

"Excuse me, but are these your shoes?" an elderly gentleman asked him. He held Joey's shoes by the laces. "You look like you just lost your best friend," he added.

"Naw, not really." Joey answered.

Then he brightened, " Did you see a little boy about six years old come through here a few minutes ago?"

"No, and I've been sitting on the front porch reading my paper for the past hour. We don't mind the kids cutting through our yard, but we do worry about the liability if something happens to them. So we try to keep an eye on 'em. But I haven't seen any kids today."

"Did you hear a woman calling for someone?"

"No, haven't seen or heard any women either."

Joey must have shown his disappointment.

"Is this boy lost?" the gentleman asked.

"No, I don't even know him. He asked me to help get his boat back, and then he disappeared when his mother called him."

The man had a curious look on his face. "Is that his boat?"

"Yes," Joey replied.

"May I see it?"

Joey handed it to him. The man turned it over. He examined it from all angles.

"I used to make boats like this when I was a boy. We would come here to visit my grandparents and I'd sneak down to the bay to sail them. In fact, I remember once . . . "his voice trailed off and he looked in the direction of the water. He looked back at Joey curiously.

"Where did you say you found this?"

"In the water, just behind the house."

They both stood there silently for a minute. The old man said, "I'm Bob Martin." He extended his hand to Joey.

"Joey Johnson." Joey shook his hand. They looked at each other closely. Joey wanted to ask him more questions, but just then the woman from the back yard came around to the front.

"Oh, hello dear. Did you find your friend?" she asked.

"No, afraid not," Joey replied.

"Well, it looks like you got a fine looking boat out of the deal." Mr. Martin handed it back to Joey.

"Yeah, a little souvenir. I better go. My mother will be wondering what happened to me." He put on his shoes.

"Thanks for bringing me my shoes."

"Not at all. They're not my size anyway," the man joked.

Joey got up to leave when an idea struck him. He knew it sounded crazy, but if he didn't ask, he'd always wonder.

"Mr. Martin, do you mind if I ask you a question?"

"Well, sounds like you just did," he replied and elbowed his wife in the ribs.

"No, I mean, ah, it might sound a bit odd, but I have my reasons."

"Sure, shoot," the old man replied.

"You said your name was Bob. Does that mean your real name is Robert?"

"Yes."

"Were you ever called Robbie?"

The smile on Mr. Martin's face disappeared. He took a swallow and then shook his head and rubbed his chin.

"I haven't been called that in more than sixty years," he answered. "And the crazy thing is only my mother called me that. My father was in the military and always insisted I be called by my full name . . . when he wasn't around though, she would call me Robbie."

Joey studied his face. *Could it be this is the Robbie I met by the water?* he thought. *Could it be that I can see people from the past, as well as hear them? Or is there a real Robbie somewhere in St. Augustine wondering what happened to his boat?*

Joey decided he didn't care. Some things can't be explained. He came here to try to figure it all out, but now he knew that would probably never happen. Whatever it was that was happening to him was like an adventure.

"I've got to go now. It was nice meeting you," he said to the Martins.

"Nice meeting you, Joey. Come back anytime," Mr. Martin said with a wink.

As Joey walked back to meet his family, somehow he knew there would be many more adventures in his future. At least, he hoped so.

THE END

Other Books by Jane R. Wood

Adventures on Amelia Island:
A Pirate, A Princess, and Buried Treasure

This book continues the escapades of the Johnson family. Local legends and tales of ghosts add to a story filled with colorful characters, humorous situations and a youthful spirit of adventure.

Finalist for a 2008 Benjamin Franklin Award

Price: $8.99   132 Pages
ISBN: 978-0-9792304-0-0

Trouble on the St. Johns River

After a close encounter with a manatee, a visit to a sea turtle center, and a family river tour, Joey, Bobby and Katy decide to "do something" to try to make a difference in protecting endangered animals and preserving the environment.

Price: $8.99   156 Pages
ISBN: 978-0-9792304-4-8

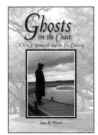

Ghosts on the Coast: A Visit to Savannah and the Low Country

It seems wherever they go, adventure follows the Johnson family. This time it comes when they visit the historic cities of Savannah, Charleston and Pawleys Island, South Carolina – cities rich in history and ghost stories!

Price: $8.99   163 Pages
ISBN: 978-0-9792304-6-2

All of Jane R. Wood's books may be ordered through
www.janewoodbooks.com

About the Author

Jane R. Wood is a former schoolteacher who enjoys writing stories for kids set in locations rich in history. *Voices in St. Augustine* is her first book. While her two sons were growing up, she often took them to St. Augustine to see the historical celebrations and re-enactments. Today she still enjoys strolling through the picturesque streets of the old city.

Mrs. Wood has also been a newspaper writer and television producer. She lives in Jacksonville, Florida, not far from "the Nation's Oldest City." You can learn more about her at www.janewoodbooks.com.